SIR SCALY PANTS

Bloomsbury Publishing, London, Oxford, New York, New Delhi and Sydney

First published in Great Britain in 2017 by Bloomsbury Publishing Plc
50 Bedford Square, London WC1B 3DP

www.bloomsbury.com

BLOOMSBURY is a registered trademark of Bloomsbury Publishing Plc

Text and illustrations copyright © John Kelly 2017

The moral rights of the author/illustrator have been asserted

A CIP catalogue record of this book is available from the British Library

ISBN 978 1 4088 5605 5 (HB)
ISBN 978 1 4088 5606 2 (PB)
ISBN 9781 4088 5604 8 (eBook)

All papers used by Bloomsbury Publishing are natural, recyclable products
from wood grown in well managed forests. The manufacturing processes
conform to the environmental regulations of the country of origin

Printed in China by Leo Paper Products, Heshan, Guangdong

1 3 5 7 9 10 8 6 4 2

OGRE PICKS A FIGHT!

OUR HERO

To everyone who has
never had a book
dedicated to them.

John Kelly

SCALY SCARES BOGEY MAN AWAY!

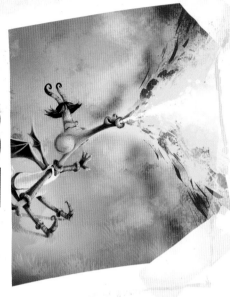

HORSEY HEROINE

sir Scaly Pants
and the
Dragon
Thief

BLOOMSBURY

LONDON OXFORD NEW YORK NEW DELHI SYDNEY

THE STORY SO FAR . . .

When Scaly Pants was just an egg
a brave and noble knight
raised the dragon as his very own
and taught him how to fight.

He graduated from Knight School
– first in his class, of course.
Then set off for adventures
on brave Guinevere, his horse.

He beat a smelly giant
when other knights had run,
and with his fiery breath
became the King's new champion!

His fame spread through the land –
"Sir Scaly fights for what is right!"
But it was quite lonely being
the one and only Dragon Knight.

One day the King
and Queen stopped by
the river for a paddle.

When suddenly...

...a DRAGON

plucked the King
out of his saddle.

It flew away, towards the east,
its claws clamped on the King.

"My true love gone!" the Queen sobbed out.
"Abducted by that thing!"

What a dreadful thing to do!
It made Sir Scaly mad.
He couldn't understand why
other dragons were SO BAD.

"Don't worry, Ma'am!" said Scaly.
"I'll ride out on Guinevere.
We will find the naughty dragon's tower
and bring our King back here!"

They saddled up
and headed east
but **every** single day,
they managed to get **lost**
and had to **stop**
to **ask** the way.

A **friendly** cyclops spied them
and then came to their assistance.
He said, "I know it's **that-a-way** . . .
but I'm not sure of the **distance**."

A **warty** woman
dressed in black said,
"Yeeeeesssss,
this is the roooute!
And would you like to
try some **broth**?
It's made from
eye of newt."

Then finally
a long-haired lady pointed,
"OVER THERE!
And would you kindly
MOVE YOUR HORSE?
She's standing on my HAIR!"

KEEP OUT

The Dragon Tower was **tall** and **dark** and on its very **top**, the **King** was **tied** securely to a flagpole – by a **knot**.

The dragon blocked the **only** gate.
He grinned and said, "Hello.
If you've got one **tonne** of **gold**,
I'll let His Highness **go**."

"You'll get **no gold**, you **dragon thief**!"
Sir Scaly Pants declared.
"So let your **nostrils** do their **worst**!
My horse and I aren't **scared**."

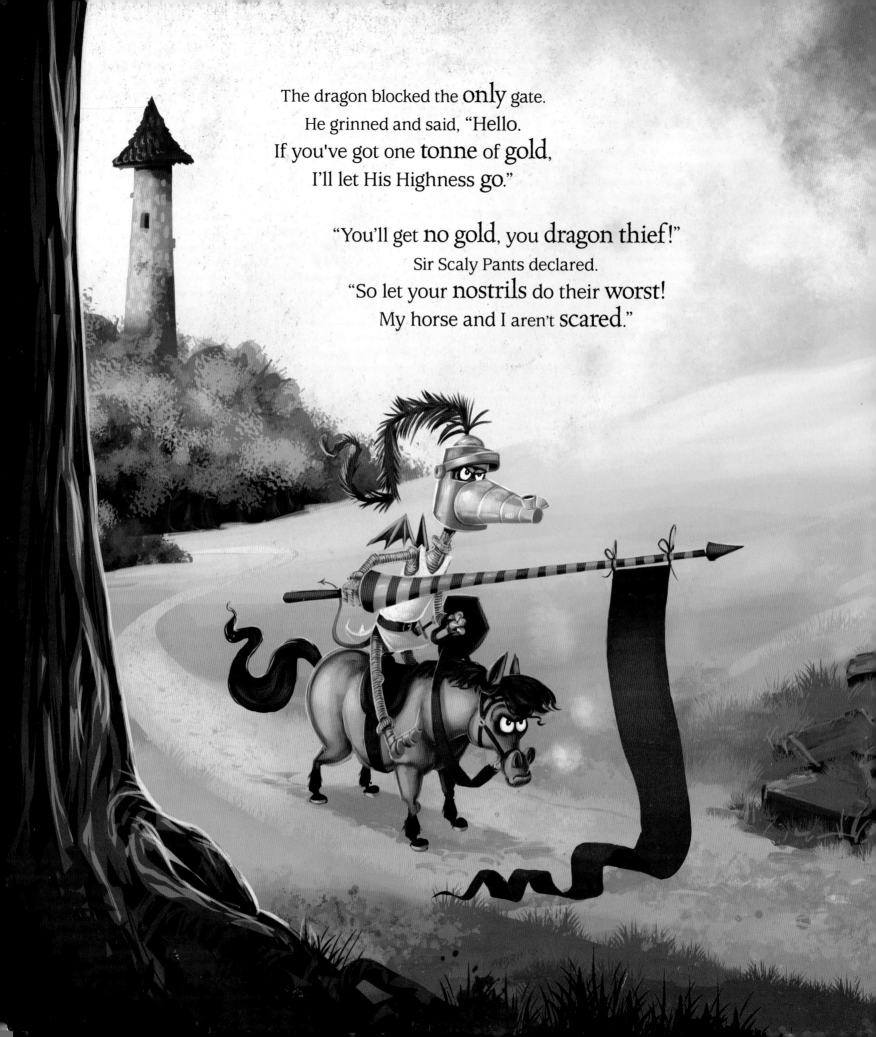

Sir Scaly shouted,
"**CHAAAARGE!**"
and Gwinny **galloped** for the tower.
But the dragon snorted **flames**
of quite unprecedented **power**.

So Gwinny swerved,

she **dodged**,

she **ducked** –

and then without a pause . . .

she **turned**
and **galloped**
straight towards . . .

the **dragon's**
open **jaws!**

"Uh-oh!" cried Scaly Pants
and hung on grimly to his horse.
For Guinevere had come up with
a CRAZY plan, of course!

She leapt OVER the head and
tiptoed down between its wings . . .

then off the tail,
and galloped
up the stairs to
save the King.

Gwinny's tiny little **hooves**
climbed **up** one thousand stairs.

She **huffed** and **puffed**
and **wheezed** and **groaned**
till they were **finally** there.

Scaly stood before the King.
"You're **safe**, Your Majesty."
While Gwinny **nibbled** through his ropes
and tried to **set him free**.

The dragon **swooped** up from below.

"Not so fast!"
he roared.
And from his nostrils
burning streams
of dragon **fire** poured!

But Scaly's shield was fireproof –
and split the fiery blast,
to save the King and Gwinny
where they huddled by the mast.

"This helmet's getting stuffy!"
said Sir Scaly with a cough.
So as the Dragon's flames ran out . . .

...Sir Scaly **whipped** it off!

The smoke cleared to reveal
Sir Scaly's thick, green, dragon skin.
The dragon gasped in disbelief.

"You're Scaly Pants!
YOU'RE HIM!"

He said, "I thought that shiny armour
meant you were a man.
I'd never hurt YOU, Scaly Pants,
I am your

BIGGEST FAN!

I've read all of your escapades
and followed your career."
He pulled a book out – "Could I get
your autograph right HERE?"

"Of course," said Scaly, "but I don't believe I caught your name?"

The dragon said, "My name is ROARGHHHAAARGGHERRRR— but you can make it out to Flame!"

While Scaly **signed**, the King untwined
the ropes that held him **tight**,
and Flame gave up his **flag** to
Scaly Pants, the Dragon Knight.

He knelt and said, "I'm **sorry!**
Scaly, can I make amends?"

"Just fly the King
back home," he said,
"and then we'll
all be friends."